I SPY

Titles in Teen Reads:

Fascination
DANIEL BLYTHE

I Spy
DANIEL BLYTHE

New Dawn
DANIEL BLYTHE

Underworld
SIMON CHESHIRE

Dawn of the Daves
TIM COLLINS

Joke Shop
TIM COLLINS

Mr Perfect
TIM COLLINS

Painkiller
TIM COLLINS

The Locals
TIM COLLINS

Troll
TIM COLLINS

Wasteland
TIM COLLINS

Copy Cat
TOMMY DONBAVAND

Dead Scared
TOMMY DONBAVAND

Just Bite
TOMMY DONBAVAND

Home
TOMMY DONBAVAND

Kidnap
TOMMY DONBAVAND

Raven
TOMMY DONBAVAND

Ward 13
TOMMY DONBAVAND

Fair Game
ALAN DURANT

Blank
ANN EVANS

By My Side
ANN EVANS

Living the Lie
ANN EVANS

Nightmare
ANN EVANS

Insectoids
ROGER HURN

Vanishing Point
CHERYL LANYON

Jigsaw Lady
TONY LEE

Mister Scratch
TONY LEE

Noticed
TONY LEE

Stalker
TONY LEE

Death Road
JON MAYHEW

Death Wheels
JON MAYHEW

The First Martian
IAIN MC LAUGHLIN

Snow White,
Black Heart
JACQUELINE RAYNER

Silent Nation
BEVERLY SANFORD

Remember Rosie
BEVERLY SANFORD

The Wishing Doll
BEVERLY SANFORD

Billy Button
CAVAN SCOTT

Mama Barkfingers
CAVAN SCOTT

Pest Control
CAVAN SCOTT

The Changeling
CAVAN SCOTT

The Hunted
CAVAN SCOTT

Sitting Target
JOHN TOWNSEND

Deadly Mission
MARK WRIGHT

Ghost Bell
MARK WRIGHT

The Corridor
MARK WRIGHT

World Without Words
JONNY ZUCKER

Badger Publishing Limited, Oldmedow Road, Hardwick Industrial Estate, King's Lynn PE30 4JJ
Telephone: 01438 791037

www.badgerlearning.co.uk

I SPY

DANIEL BLYTHE

I Spy ISBN 978-1-78464-607-3

Publisher: Susan Ross
Senior Editor: Danny Pearson
Editorial Coordinator: Claire Morgan
Copyeditor: Cambridge Publishing Management
Designer: Bigtop Design Ltd
Cover: © 3D Stock Illustrations / Alamy Stock Photo

2 4 6 8 10 9 7 5 3 1

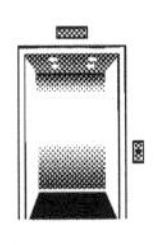

CHAPTER 1

AVALON TOWER

There are times when I think the building is watching me. It feels alive with its creaks and groans, its little judders in the high winds.

It's called Avalon Tower. A metal monster, the tallest luxury apartment block in London.

It's built out here on a wasteland, looking out across the city. They chose the site well. The people on the highest floors can look down on the city in the evening, see tiny blue and orange lights glow. The little fireflies of life, showing them where all the little people live, skulking down there in their flats and houses, far beneath them.

Bel, my mum, wants to live in Avalon Tower more than anything. It's safe to say I don't.

***

When we first came to it, driving across the strip of half-built road, I could not believe how ugly it was. Three tall cylinders of glass and steel stuck together, like something out of a sci-fi movie.

"There?" I said in disbelief. "That's the famous Avalon Tower?"

My mum's face was blank behind her sunglasses. "Don't be like that, Taz. It's very sought-after."

"I don't care. It's horrible. When you said tower I was thinking of something more like… well… a castle. Like Rapunzel's tower."

My mum allowed herself a little smile. "Don't worry, my little Rapunzel. You'll have plenty of chances to let your hair down."

"Ha ha. Very funny. I'm not a kid."

Talking of hair, Mum's is pretty jaw-dropping for a forty-year-old woman. Or thirty-nine, as she claims to be. She calls it 'galaxy hair' and it's the latest thing, she says. Glossy, full, dyed a rich blue like the night sky, with streaks of green and purple like the Northern Lights. She's a fashion designer and thinks she looks so cool. I just think she looks sad.

She also has a pierced nose. She wears crop tops and leather miniskirts and flirts with guys half her age. It is so embarrassing.

We park the car in a huge metal space. We have our own parking spot: BELINDA JESSOP, it says in sharp red letters. Mum's name. She's kept Dad's surname after all this time, even though she moans about how awful he was when they were married. Well, she found his money useful enough. She wouldn't have been able to start her business up without it.

The car door slides shut. Mum clicks her phone and the car goes tweet-tweet, flashing lights at us as it locks.

"Ready for life in the skies?" she says with a smile.

I scowl and fold my arms.

The lift is smooth, sleek, smells brand new. I slump in the corner, not looking at my mother with her stupid blue hair.

There's no going back, I know. All our stuff has been moved into the flat by a company who do that kind of thing, and I didn't have any say in any of it.

We used to live in Eastford, a little town in Hampshire where I knew everyone. I went to Vale Crest High, the local comprehensive, and I could hang around down town and always see someone I knew. But Mum sold the cottage and we've had to move to this place, because Mum thinks it's better for her career. Seriously? She designs clothes and writes fashion books. Can't she do that anywhere? I've got to go to some stupid private school in London now. I'm a two-hour train ride away from Grace, Tom, Halima and all my other mates in Eastford.

I really hate my mother right now.

"You're bound to make some friends," she says. The lift doors swish shut and we start to climb — smoothly, almost silently. "There are lots of families here. And there's an indoor park on Floor 10. You can go there and play."

"Play?" I snap in disgust, turning even further away from her into the corner of the lift. She sometimes talks to me like I am ten, not sixteen.

Doors swish open on to the twentieth floor lobby. It is sleek, all shining metal and glass, lined with green ferns. It seems to have no soul. One wall has AVALON on it in giant red letters. There are leather sofas and steel tables everywhere, and a huge water cooler lit from beneath in icy blue. I hate the place already.

It smells new, like fresh paint. People say the Queen thinks everywhere smells of new paint because everywhere she visits gets a fresh coat of gloss the day before she arrives. I suppose that's quite funny, really. Not that I'm in the mood for a laugh right now.

There are four apartments on each floor. Ours is Apartment 104. There's a keypad on what looks like an old-fashioned wooden door. My mum taps the code in and the wooden door, rather than swinging back, slides quietly open. Mum steps back, clapping her hands with delight.

"Oh, *awesome*!" she exclaims.

I sigh and fold my arms. "I can't even begin to tell you how sad it is having you for a mother," I say.

"Thank you, sweetie. I love you too." My mother laughs and swishes her glittering hair. "Shall we go in?"

Just before I step inside, I glance over my shoulder, taking another look around the lobby.

I see someone hovering on the far side, over by one of the big plants. A boy with red hair and blue glasses, pretending to look at one of the magazines but not doing a very good job of it.

I stare at him and he ducks behind the magazine, like a toddler hiding from its parents. As if he thinks this makes him invisible.

***

All right, so in one way I can't really complain. It's one of the most beautiful luxury flats you could ever hope to live in — if that's the kind of thing you like.

Everything seems to be either jet-black or snow-white. White-tiled floors, smooth white walls, black furniture and glossy black wooden doors. There are those stupid bowls of black pebbles with candles in them everywhere, like you see in the magazines my mum reads.

My mother prances around, clapping her hands and plumping up cushions. "Isn't this wonderful?"

"Yeah. *Wonderful.*" I don't think she even notices I am being sarcastic.

So, here's what we've got.

A huge lounge with floors on three levels, massive sofas and a 60-inch HD-TV. There's a huge picture window looking out west across the city, so you can watch the sunset. You can tint the glass at the touch of a button, even make it go dark at night. No need for curtains.

I've got a huge bedroom with a massive bed, tablet, TV and a walk-in wardrobe full of new clothes. I've got my own en-suite bathroom with a jacuzzi and another TV, a splash-proof one, built into the wall. There are art prints on all the walls, and the soft lighting is somehow *inside* the walls and ceilings, like clouds of light in a black sky.

I flop down on my huge soft bed and stare at the coal-black ceiling with its built-in spotlights.

"But it's all so *horrible!*" I say out loud.

This is my mum's palace, her perfect home. It tells her she has arrived in the world. She didn't even think about me.

***

I don't start at school for a couple of weeks, so I've got some time to do whatever I want.

On our second day, I ride the lift up and down, stopping at random floors. They all look the same, although I discover the park on Floor 10. A huge square of astro-turf beneath a giant sweep of curved glass — pretending to be in the open air.

There's more play equipment than I've seen in any adventure playground. There are, as far as I can see, three kids running round. There's a blonde girl of about seven on the swings, being watched (sort of) by her bored, bearded dad. He seems more interested in his phone. Meanwhile, a young mum in a hijab is spinning two boys on the designer steel merry-go-round.

I wander around, pretending to look at my phone and occasionally at the view. I see the young mum smiling at me, and I smile back. Her two kids are about ten and eleven, though. Where are all the people my age?

At least the kids' squeals and laughs seem happy enough. Then I hear how they echo up to the top of the big glass bubble and they suddenly sound lost and lonely, like the cries of seagulls on the shore.

It's so sad that I get back in the lift and press the button for the basement.

The lift doors swish open to reveal a smooth, empty swimming pool.

The water is flat and calm, as if nobody has ever touched it. Huge soft round lights line the walls. Their reflections barely wobble in the smooth water. There are sofas all along both sides, and there's a Roman mosaic on the far wall. There's a strong smell of chlorine, and it's so humid here I feel myself sweating straightaway. I step out of the lift, pulling my hoodie off and tying it around my waist.

I pace the length of the pool and realise this is a full Olympic-size one, fifty metres. There's nobody around. I sit down on the edge of the pool and trail my fingers in the cool water, watching the ripples in the surface.

"Boring," I say out loud. "Seriously, so boring."

"Dull, isn't it?"

I jump to my feet, looking round wildly. I almost slip over, but I grab hold of one of the sofas just in time.

I can't see anyone else in the pool. But it was definitely a young male voice, and it came from nearby.

"Where are you?" I demand. I'm looking up and down, my voice echoing off every wall. "I can't see you!"

"I know," says the voice, and it sounds as if it finds all of this really funny. *"But you know what, Taz? I can see you."*

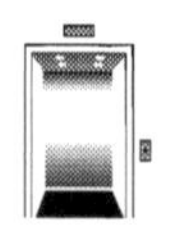

CHAPTER 2

FLOOR 41

"All right, this is really creepy. Stop it." I fold my arms and scowl.

"You want me to stop it? But you were only just saying how bored you were!"

Even in the humidity, a chill goes up my spine. "How do you know my name? Who the hell are you?"

"You want to know?" says the voice. *"Come up to Floor 41."*

"Don't be stupid. There is no Floor 41."

"That's what you think!"

I realise, now, where the voice is coming from. There's a speaker in the wall behind one of the sofas. It's half hidden by another of those giant potted ferns which are all over the place.

"The floors in the lift only go up to 40," I say. "I'm kind of observant like that."

"Maybe not observant enough. Look in the back pocket of your jeans."

Frowning, a little fearful, I reach into my pocket. My fingers close over a slim plastic card, the size and shape of a credit card.

I pull it out, staring at it and turning it over. It is matte black, plain on one side apart from a magnetic strip. The other side has the bright red A of the Avalon Tower logo on it.

"What's this?" I ask. "How did it get here?"

"Put it in the slot under the lift-buttons," says the voice. *"It's your ticket to Floor 41."*

I fold my arms and glare at the speaker-grille. "Suppose I don't want to come to Floor 41?"

Soft mocking laughter from the grille. *"Oh, but you do, Taz. You won't be able to resist it."*

"Tell me who you are first!" I shout angrily.

But there's no response. My mystery man has either gone or decided not to say any more.

I stand there in the humid chlorine-smelling air, listening to the building creaking and whirring all around me.

I take a decision. I call the lift, which seems to take much longer than it did earlier on. I watch the numbers counting down.

15, 14, 13…

But I'm suddenly really unsettled, here on my own in the empty, unused swimming hall where a ghostly voice spoke to me.

I flip the card over and over between my fingers. I'm tempted just to chuck it in the water and forget about it.

7, 6, 5….

I stare at the red A on the card. It looks official. Whoever the voice was, he said it could get me up to Floor 41. And since I didn't even know there *was* a Floor 41 until a few minutes ago, I'm now desperate to find out what's there.

4, 3, 2…

I know what I am going to do.

The lift reaches the basement. A loud *ping* sounds as the doors swish open for me. I step inside. Sure enough, as the voice said, there's a slot under the panel of numbered buttons for the floors. It's just the right size to take the card.

I hold the card out between thumb and forefinger and cautiously slide it into the slot. A millisecond later, it feels as if the card is grabbed from my hand by something inside the slot, and the lift doors swish shut.

“Override enabled,” says a soft recorded female voice. “Ascending to penthouse.”

Penthouse? Right. That sounds interesting.

Here we go, then.

The lift seems to sail even more smoothly up the tower. Somehow, I know it isn’t going to stop at any other floors until we get there.

I watch the numbers climbing: 19, 20, 21. Past my floor and beyond. My mum will be in our flat, right now, designing or writing or meeting with clients or whatever else she is doing today. 30, 31, 32. Up, up we go, right up to the top.

As we reach 40, the lift seems to slow. It judders, machinery squeals. Terrified, I press myself against the back wall of the lift, keeping my eyes fixed on the digital readout of the floor numbers.

The lift climbs the last floor.

Slowly. Unbearably slowly. And then — *ping*.

The doors swish open, and I step into Floor 41.

***

The first thing I notice is that it's colder up here, and darker. It smells new, like plastic. The lobby looks like every other floor's lobby, only this one is lit in blue, making it look cold and unwelcoming.

The sofas and water coolers are covered in thick sheets of plastic. The walls are a dull grey, rather than white, as if someone didn't get beyond painting the undercoat.

I can always turn round and go back, I suppose.

The card pops out of its slot, making me jump.

"Take it," says the voice.

This time, it's talking to me from the speaker in the lift. I almost expected that, so I am not so startled this time. I obey, taking the card and tucking it into the pocket of my jeans again.

"Which way do I go?" I ask.

"*You can't get lost,*" says the voice. "*There's only one apartment on this floor. Just walk straight ahead.*"

And I realise the voice is right. Unlike those on the other floors, this lobby doesn't have exits leading off it to different landings and the doors of various apartments. Instead, it's just a big open grey space. There's one solid pair of polished black doors in front of me.

I walk across the floor, my footsteps clicking. At first I stay in the pool of light from the lift. Then, of course, the lift doors rumble shut, and the pool of light becomes a bar of light, then a thinner bar, then nothing.

The lift doors shut with a thud.

On the other side of the lobby, I put a hand to the black doors in front of me. To my surprise, they slide open at my touch. Inside, I step on to a thick blue carpet. The walls are a deep red. It's dimly lit in here as well, but in warm orange. There's a welcoming spicy aroma like lemon and cinnamon. The carpet gives way to a flight of shiny jet-black steps.

I can hear water.

I step into a space about the size of a school hall. The floor is made up of glossy dark squares of some expensive wood. It has a high vaulted ceiling with a fan slowly swishing around. *Whoosh, whoosh.* Dead centre of the floor is a small fountain, splashing merrily on a rockery and lit softly from below.

Beyond that, another door slides open.

And then he's there, leaning against the door frame, jauntily smiling.

One of the fittest guys I have ever seen.

Tall, with thick dark hair swept back from his tanned face. Dark blue eyes. High cheekbones and a cheeky mouth. He's lean and muscular, in a tight white T-shirt, black designer jeans and red sneakers. Understated, cool and he knows it.

Behind him, down another short flight of steps, I can see another room, even darker than this one, but with a strange blue light flickering across the floor.

"Hi there," he says, sounding as if he finds the whole thing really funny. "I'm Luke, and I've been expecting you. Tasmin Jessop, right?"

I blink, swallow hard, and stop at a safe distance from him. Hands on hips, I try to look assertive. "Taz," I say.

"Yup. I know. Your mum designs some of the stuff my mum wears. Writes for the magazines she reads too."

It's a bit creepy that he knows my name.

"*Your* mum?" I say cautiously. The flickering blue light behind Luke is really odd, making him look like a ghost or a demon.

"Yeah. Eva Horton. You've probably heard of her."

Probably heard of her? Oh, my God. Eva Horton is only the star of the biggest show on TV right now, *Imperatrix*. A sci-fi version of the Roman Empire. Six seasons, so far. This is surreal.

"I've… watched her show," I say, cautiously, still not quite able to believe this is real. "Every episode's online."

Luke grins. His teeth are perfect and white. "Enjoy it while it lasts. They kill her off this season."

My jaw drops in outrage. "Oh, spoiler? Thanks!"

"You're welcome," he says.

"I… didn't know she had a son."

"Yeah. She doesn't advertise the fact. She and my dad are divorced. They don't get on. In fact, she hates his guts. And sometimes I remind her that he exists — which is kind of inconvenient in the circles she moves in."

Silence, for a moment, apart from the splashing of the fountain. Eventually, I say, "Why did you invite me up here? How do I know it's safe? What do you want?"

Luke ticks off the answers on his fingers, mocking me again. "Well, in order: I was bored, you don't, and…. *fun*." He gestures inside the room. "Want to come and see the big secret of Avalon Tower?"

"Big secret? What do you mean?"

"Come on. I'll show you."

I'm cautious now. "My mum doesn't know I'm here."

He shrugs. "You can call her if you like. Or just turn around and walk out. Up to you. I'm not keeping you here." He presses a button on his phone, and behind me the main entrance doors to the lobby slide open again. "Shall I call the lift for you?"

"No," I say, perhaps too quickly. "All right. I'll come and look."

"That's the spirit," he says with a wicked grin.

I follow him down the steps into the room beyond.

It's a curved chamber with almost nothing in it apart from a metal desk — covered in magazines, used plates and cups. On the left, a giant round picture window looks out over the city. It's tinted green, soft on the eyes.

There's a small laptop on the desk, and two leather swivel chairs. On the wall is the biggest bank of flickering TV screens I've ever seen. I stand there, mouth gaping, counting them. Sixteen rows up, and twenty rows across. That's... I screw my face up, working it out...

"Three hundred and twenty," says Luke.

I stare at him. "You knew what I was trying to work out."

He shrugs, sprawls in one of the big leather chairs, feet up on the desk. "Pretty obvious," he says. "So — what do you think?"

I suddenly realise what I am looking at.

The screens are not showing TV programmes. They are showing images of all the public places in Avalon Tower. Corridors. The lobby. The playground. The car park where we arrived. All picked out in smooth, crisp pixels. Full colour too. I'm looking at a bank of closed-circuit HD-TV screens.

I'm standing here in the penthouse, with Luke Horton, and I'm looking at three hundred and twenty windows on to the Tower.

Three hundred and twenty spy-cams.

CHAPTER 3

SECURITY

I gawp at the screens. I'm standing in their flickering light, realising I must look a bit stupid with my mouth wide open. Gormless. I shut my mouth, shrug and slump onto Luke's other chair.

"So… you some kind of caretaker here, then, or what?" I ask him.

Even as soon as I say it, I realise it's a stupid thing to say. What would Eva Horton's son be doing working as a caretaker? It's not like he needs the money.

I'm keeping him at a distance, really worried that he knows my name. Was he watching me down in the pool? And elsewhere too?

Luke Horton laughs. "Yeah. Caretaker. I like that. I take care of a lot of things, for sure."

I don't like his smugness, now. "All right. So what are you?"

"I'm me," he says. "Luke. And, thanks to darling Mummy, I can do whatever the hell I like."

"Oh, up yourself much?"

He spreads his hands. "If you like to think so." He claps his hands together and stares at me over them, his eyes bright and sharp. "It wasn't always like this, you know. Mum wasn't always rich. Not before *Imperatrix*."

I blush. "I s'pose I'd never really thought about it like that."

"She was really struggling after Dad left. She was doing stupid little plays in local theatres, Godforsaken places like Barnsley or somewhere. And TV and radio ads and voiceovers, and some bar work, all just to pay the rent. I've lost track of how many different schools I went to. She found it hard, you know. Yeah, she got a lucky break in the end, a massive one. But she worked hard. She deserved it."

"OK. Sorry. I'm not dissing your mum."

He smiles, toying with the keyboard and making some of the images zoom and twirl. "All right. It's just that some of these actors, you know... They're born with a silver spoon up them. They can afford to muck about on Daddy's money while they wait for the big break. Not my mum. She's from East London, from a council estate."

I think about Eva Horton's posh, classy vowels. "You wouldn't know it," I tell him.

"Well, yeah, course not. She's had voice training and all that. Got to, haven't you? In case some corsets-and-horses drama comes along and you've got to talk all plummy to impress some poncy little director called Tarquin."

I smile at him. I picture a Tarquin, all big gestures and a ponytail, and probably yellow trousers. This, at least, makes me laugh.

"So what's all this?" I ask him, gesturing at the screens and leaning forward. "Are you what they used to call a Peeping Tom?"

"Just security, really."

"Oh, come on. Security? Seriously?"

Luke's hand trails across the keypad and the screen in the top right enlarges to fill all the screens. It's an image of the car park, still pin-sharp. I realise, now, that they are not separate monitors, but just a sort of digital chequer-board on one big hi-res screen. So he can set it to show as many or as few images at a time as he likes.

"There are cameras everywhere in the building," he says. "And I know exactly where they all are, because my stepfather designed it."

"You're kidding me."

"You can check. David Marston, award-winning architect. No?"

OK, so I have to confess I hadn't remembered, if indeed I ever knew. David Marston isn't Eva's current husband, I know that much. It was all over the papers when she left him for her younger co-star in *Desolate Frontier*. And that didn't last. She's just married a nu-metal singer ten years younger than her — Kai Darien of Awaken Chaos. They got matching tattoos instead of rings.

I expect it may not be a good idea to mention this to Luke. I'm not sure how he feels about having a new stepdad who's not much older than him. I try another tack.

"So, what — I'm expected to believe your dad just told you everything about the building?"

"Stepdad. Not exactly. I got the plans off his rather poorly-protected laptop. Well, poorly-protected if you happen to be an IT genius like me."

I snort with scorn. "Modest too! No end to your talents, is there?"

Luke grins. He doesn't seem bothered about anything I say. "Want to play around with it?" he asks.

"What, me?"

"There's nobody else here."

Luke talks me through the set-up — how to toggle between the cameras, how to zoom in and out. He shows me the few cameras in the building with a 360-degree spin. They're the ones which hang from the ceilings in the public places, little upside-down black domes on rods. It's all quite easy when you get the hang of it.

"The hilarious thing is," Luke says, opening a can of fizzy drink and offering me one, "the security's a big selling point here. And they're happy with being watched — in the car parks, hallways and the public spaces, like the park and the botanical garden."

"Botanical garden?" That's a new one on me. "Where's that?"

"Floor 8. They're even talking about people having *allotments* there. Mini-greenhouses where they can grow stuff. Should get the organic-obsessed diet types flooding in." Luke's tone, I've noticed, always sounds like he's joking but also sneering.

"So," I say slowly, flicking through image after image of stairwells and dull landings and corridors, "how does this get interesting?"

I want to know where else the cameras are. I'm convinced he isn't telling me everything.

Luke grins. "Ah, well," he says, "maybe that's for next time."

"Next time?"

"You want to come back, don't you?"

I'm confused. "Yes, but..."

"You should go back to your mum," he says. He taps the keyboard and all the screens darken.

"Seriously?"

Luke smiles at me. "You're curious. And there's nothing else going on for you in this place — is there?"

I shrug. "I wouldn't say that."

"Admit it. You're bored." Luke grins. "Look — come back, OK?" His face is suddenly serious and adult. "But don't just come when you feel like it. I've given you that card as a privilege. Don't abuse it. You wait to be invited, right?"

Who does he think he is, bossing me about like this? I ought to get mad with him, ought to sound off, go and give him a shove. But I don't.

I smile, shrug again.

"OK," I say. "I'll wait."

"Good girl," he says.

Yeah, I should feel patronised. But I don't.

CHAPTER 4

MOTHER AND DAUGHTER

Luke's words ring in my ears over the next day or two. *There's nothing else going on for you in this place — is there?*

What's different, now, though is — well, several things.

I know there is a Floor 41. I keep the plastic card in a zip-pocket of my jeans and I even sleep with it under my pillow at night. And when I'm out on the landing, in the swimming-pool, in the park, I look up. I see one of the little black half-globes coming down from the ceiling on its extendable stick. Polished, dark, smooth, with just a glowing red light inside. And I know he may well be watching me.

It should feel creepy, but it doesn't.

It makes me feel needed and wanted.

***

"Have you made any friends yet?" says my mother, as she serves us bowls of risotto at the polished granite table.

I shrug. "Not really. There aren't any other people my age around, are there? I've just seen little kids in the park."

"Well, it'll be different when you start school. I've been looking at a few places," she says.
Her ridiculous hair shimmers as she sits down. She pours herself a large white wine in a tall blue glass.

"Really?" I say awkwardly.

I don't really want to think about school. It's only been a few weeks since I made a complete hash of my exams. Well, the results aren't out until August, so I don't know, but I can guess. The fact that I wrote I DON'T KNOW, I DON'T CARE all over most of my second Maths paper is unlikely to have got me any kind of grade. Although, who knows? They may give me a grade E out of sympathy.

I haven't told Mum that, yet. I haven't told her about walking out of Geography to cry in the toilets, either. That won't have left many options. Oh, and French? I didn't turn up. I just told her I did my best, and she seemed to believe me.

The only one I actually know I did OK in is Art. I *know* I can draw. I don't take as much pleasure in it as I used to.

"So, what do you think?" Mum says.

I realise she wants an answer. I stare at the three brochures on the table. They all look similar. Shiny, glossy girls with hockey sticks, books and chemistry flasks, against a backdrop of ivy-covered stone buildings. Even the names of the places are similar. Saint This, Saint That, Saint Something Else.

I leaf through the heavy glossy pages while eating. They are all private girls' schools somewhere just outside London. They all look really horrible.

"The thing about all of these," Mum says, "is that they're all good value for money, offer *marvellous* opportunities and they can take people at short notice. Right up to September."

"Can't I just go back to Vale Crest? Halima, Tom and Grace have all said they're staying on."

"Yes, well," says my mother, and allows the comment to sit there.

It's unsaid, but I know what she's thinking. My small-town comprehensive, Vale Crest High, old and unloved, weird but comfy in its own way, is *fine for the likes of Halima, Tom and Grace.* She doesn't even have to say it. I can hear it in her voice. She's never thought much of my friends from Eastford. Never even tried to disguise it.

I thought my mum was meant to have been cool when she was young. I wonder when she became such a snob?

I've heard rumours about my mum. About teenage Bel. That she was what my Grandad Jon calls 'a bit of a tearaway' twenty years ago in the coastal town where she grew up. Joyriding, drugs, I think, stuff like that. Trouble with the police too, even though she was never done for anything. You wouldn't know it now.

I've asked Grandad Jon to tell me more, but he just smiles and says, "What's past is past, Tasmin," and refuses to talk about it.

But I doubt, even with all that in mind, that she'd think much of my messing my exams up quite so badly. I'm not sure she'd be that impressed by my friendship — if you can call it that — with Luke, either.

Oh, and I've tried finding him online. I wasn't all that surprised to find that he doesn't have a profile anywhere. No Instagram, no Twitter, no Facebook. I even thought of hacking my mum's LinkedIn to see if he's on there, and then I told myself not to be so tragic.

"I don't like any of them."

There's no point in trying to hide it. She would find out sooner or later anyway.

"Really, darling?"

"Really. I hate them all, Bel. I want to go back to Vale Crest."

I call Mum by her first name when I want to be taken seriously. As an adult.

She purses her lips and peers over her glasses,

in a way that makes her look much older than thirty-nine or forty or whatever she is.

"Give yourself some time to think about it," she says. "I'm doing well in life, Taz. I can afford the best for you, you know. Some of these places send dozens of girls to Oxford and Cambridge every year."

"So? What's that got to do with me? I'm not going there. Last I looked, they didn't take thickos."

"Don't you dare call yourself that. You've been under-achieving because of your… problems, that's all."

I push the remains of the risotto away and sit back, arms folded. "You think you can solve everything by throwing money at it."

My mother seems to think this over, twirling her glasses around between thumb and forefinger.

"No," she says at last, "not really. But I do think it helps. It can cushion the blow."

"Cushion the blow. Yeah, right. Anyway, what would you know? You didn't exactly grow up poor."

"No. But… I had difficulties later. Made bad decisions, lost a lot of money. Got in with the wrong people for a while. And then I sorted my life out, and made a success of myself."

"You were in the nuthouse," I sneer.

Mum shrinks back at my horrible, un-PC word. I'm not even sorry. I actually enjoy hurting her sometimes.

"You were, though, weren't you?" I say. "In your twenties. Before you had me. You dropped out of uni, went crazy for a bit."

My mother puts her glasses on, and very slowly gets up and walks to the window. She presses the remote control, dimming the glass against the glowing London sunset.

Despite myself, I think she still looks good for her age. The hair is a bit much, but she's wearing a tailored jacket and jeans that look very nice on her. She's slim and toned, but then you'd expect that. Kev, her personal trainer, comes in every morning at eight to put her through an hour of exercises. I hear her gasping and hitting the punch-bag when I'm still trying to have a lie-in.

"Yes, Taz," she says softly. "Yes, I had a… Well, I had an incident. A psychotic episode. I was convinced someone was trying to kill me. It was pretty horrible at the time." She turns and stares at me. "I must admit, I didn't think you knew. How did you find out?"

I shrug. I want to be vague. She won't like it if I tell her.

"Got my ways," I say.

"Seriously. This is not the kind of thing that you can find out through *Snapchat*." She says the name with a sneer. "So how do you know?"

A long silence. Then I decide I might as well tell her. It may take some of the heat off me.

"Kate told me."

Mum narrows her eyes, nodding as if she has had something confirmed that she suspected. "I see. As if that woman didn't do enough damage."

Kate was Grandad Jon's wife, who Mum always hated. Such a cliché — the evil stepmum. But I gather she was pretty horrible to her. Why she chose to tell me about my mother's past, I still don't know. It was six years ago at Christmas, when all the adults had knocked back quite a bit to drink. So I'd have been ten, and not quite getting why they were all more relaxed and giggly than they had been in the morning.

I didn't really understand what Kate — I never, *ever* called her Granny Kate — was talking about at the time, but I've processed it since. I put two and two together, as they say.

Kate died of cancer a couple of years ago. She was only, like, fifty-seven or something. I remember Mum could not even pretend to be sorry at the time.

"So," she says, leaning on the table. "You know I'm not perfect." She plants a kiss on my forehead. "Think about the schools thing for me, Taz. Please."

I make a non-committal noise.

"Look," she says, glancing at her watch, "I've got a Skype conference with New York. Why don't you take your sketchbook out and about? You've hardly touched it since we arrived."

***

On my bed, I stare at the ceiling, thinking about Luke. Wondering why he's doing all this. And deciding that he doesn't need a reason. Luke's just a bored rich kid. Other bored rich kids fill their time with parties and drugs and shopping. He either doesn't need any of that, or he's moved on from it already.

I'm not sure if I actually *like* him, but he's the one intriguing thing about Avalon Tower so far.

My sketchbook, with its green cover, is sitting beside me on the bedside table. Taunting me, almost. I pick it up, leaf through it, allowing my hand to stroke the smooth, clean pages.

I swing round, sit on the edge of the bed. I find my pencils in a drawer and head off out.

The landing is dark and unwelcoming. For some reason, the usual lighting has cut out. A soft orange glow comes from round panels set into the wall. I didn't even realise they were there — they are invisible when the normal lights are on.

Shadows lurk in the corners. I look up and down, and it doesn't take me long to spot a camera. In the ceiling, at the junction of two corridors.

I go and stand under it, sketchbook clutched to me. As it swivels round towards me, I give it a little wave.

I know something nobody else knows.

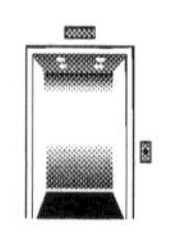

CHAPTER 5

WATCHING

The viewing gallery is on Floor 27. A huge open space. You can see from end to end, blue-tinted glass all round.

There is a walkway made of shiny wood, with digital information points explaining what you can see out of the window. The clouds are fiery in the light of the setting sun.

In the middle of the floor is a random-looking array of big wooden cylinders, cones and other shapes, each about the height of a person. It's a sort of exhibition. They've got black and white photos on them showing the history and building of Avalon Tower.

Of course, Floor 41 isn't mentioned.

I sit down on a bench with my sketchbook and a soft pencil, and try to decide on the best way to approach this.

After ten minutes, I've captured a rough outline of the shapes, benches and curved windows, with a hint of the city outside. It's how I like to work. I do a rough, ragged impression in the softest pencil, leaving all my mistakes in, spiky edges all around. I usually manage to see the shape I want begin to emerge.

I look up, checking the perspective.

That's when I see him.

He darts behind one of the big cones, but not quickly enough. I have spotted him. A flash of red hair, a glint of blue glasses.

I close my book, stick my pencil behind my ear and march over to him. There's no way I can do it stealthily on the wooden floor. My footsteps echo all around.

I circle the cone and see him trying to dart off. I head the other way and grab him by his arm, twisting him round. He squeals like an animal and wrenches free, standing there rubbing his arm and glowering at me.

"What did you do that for?" he mumbles. He's one of those boys who doesn't quite look you in the eye, I notice. He doesn't properly open his mouth when he speaks.

"You been spying on me, Ginger?" I ask him.

"Nah."

"I saw you when I arrived," I say. "Skulking in the hallway."

"Yeah, so? Last time I checked that wasn't illegal."

I suppose he's right. I look him up and down. He's scrawny, freckly, wears thick glasses, and it's hard to tell how old he is. He could be anywhere between fifteen and eighteen.

"What do you want?" I ask him.

He shrugs, leans against the wooden cone. "Just… don't often see new people here. That's all."

"Really? Your life must be so exciting, Ginger."

"Don't call me that. It's racist."

"It's not *racist*, you plank. I'm just insulting your hair colour." I realise I am being a bit cruel. "All right, so what's your name?"

"James."

"OK. Who do you live with, James?"

"My mum and dad. On Floor 20, just along from you. So we're neighbours."

"So what do you… do?"

"Between schools. Like you, I'm guessing." He grins. "I'm waiting to go to college. I've got a placement sponsored by LumiTech."

I don't know what that is, so I don't ask. I don't want to look stupid. "This place is so weird. Why are there so few people here?"

"My dad says it'll take a year or more to fill it up properly," says James, with an air of authority.

"Really? Why?"

"Overpriced," he says. "Not getting people who can afford it. People have seen too many of these places before." James nods, wisely. Acting older than his years.

"Maybe." I'm edging away from him, now, wanting to get back to my sketching. I don't want him thinking he's my *friend*.

"There are secrets here," James says, narrowing his eyes, as I am about to move away.

I feel myself go cold. "Secrets?" I say, keeping my voice light.

"Yeah." He lowers his voice to a whisper. "I haven't worked it all out yet, but I think it's something to do with *them*." He nods at the hovering cameras up near the ceiling.

"Oh, those? Just security, aren't they?" I am anxious to get away. But what does he know? Has he rumbled Luke? Does he know about Floor 41?

I don't get to find out, because at that moment his phone goes off. He sighs, and takes the call. "Yeah, hi Dad."

I take the opportunity, and stride towards the lift.

Again, I seem to be on my own for the lift. Inside, I wait for the doors to close, and then slide the black plastic card into the slot again.

Floor 41, here I come. I've got a few questions for Mr Luke Horton.

The lift begins to climb.

This time, though, it seems to creak and judder more than it did before. I really don't like the noises it's making. It sounds like ice creaking on a mountain, an ocean pressing down on an underwater tunnel. My heart pounding, I press myself against the wall of the lift.

Floor 31, 32, 33.

The digital display goes wild, breaking up. It looks like it's showing 88, 89, 88, 89. I have no idea if the lift is still going up. The light flickers, buzzes like a wasp. It dims to orange, then to red.

There is a big, serious THUD and the lift comes to a halt.

OK, don't panic. There will be an alarm somewhere. And I have got my phone.

I have got my phone… haven't I?

Panic rising, I'm scrabbling in my pockets. I realise my phone must be still on the dining room table.

And just then, the lights flicker back to normality and the lift starts to climb again.

Breathing a huge sigh of relief, I reach Floor 41 safely, and hurry across the cold, dark space to the black doors.

They're ajar. The soft lights are on inside as before, and the fountain is splashing in the little room beyond.

"Luke? You there?"

I go forwards, round the fountain into the room with all the CCTV screens. The screens are on, but there's no sign of Luke. The room seems huge, cold and quiet, like a cathedral.

"Luke! It's Taz. Are you in?" I call, trying to sound strong and confident.

There's an empty coffee cup on the desk, so I go and look at it — almost empty, just dregs. I clasp it in both hands. Not that warm. OK, so that proves nothing.

Silently, the CCTV screens flicker. Through the round picture window I can see the city spread out beyond, lights starting to twinkle. It's dusk.

It's then that I notice something.

My mouth open, I go and stand right underneath the screens, looking up, almost wanting to touch them, as if I can't quite believe it.

Some screens still show the dull images of car parks and outer doors, of corridors with strange shadows. Of the lift areas and the park and the viewing gallery. All the places I knew there were cameras.

But there are a few screens showing other places.

Kitchens. Living rooms. Dining rooms.

Bedrooms. The same layout as our flat, but all with subtly different decoration.

Oh, my God.

I got quite good at using the laptop before. I dart back to the keyboard and have another play around, flicking between cameras. Choosing the ones Luke didn't show me before.

It doesn't take long before I've got a grid of images showing the insides of apartments. OK, most are empty — some are unfurnished and some aren't even decorated properly. There are some with kitchens still covered in plastic sheeting, with paint pots here and there and workmen's stepladders. But the ones where people live — they stand out. The rooms are cluttered, busy.

And there are people.

I see a woman in a flowery blouse, unaware of the camera, fill the kettle at her sink and cross to the worktop to plug the kettle in. Remembering the layout of our kitchen, I'm thinking the camera must be somewhere up behind the big fridge.

A young guy is sprawled on his sofa, reading something off a laptop. A black cat trots past the camera, heading off on its own little mission. The guy turns towards the cat with a smile and, with a start, I recognise the guy now. It's Beardy Dad from the park.

This feels wrong. It feels bad. These people don't know the cameras are there.

At least... I'm assuming they don't, right? I mean — they can't, can they? Nobody would ever agree to that. Nobody would actually allow their modern, expensive apartment to become the Big Brother house.

I'm wondering how these got installed, and when. And whether the architect, Luke's stepfather, David Marston, knew about this and planned it — or if it's the doing of his smug son. I'm also wondering whether this breaks any laws.

I mean, it must do, surely?

"Hello, Taz."

His voice makes me jump. I whirl around, knocking the empty coffee cup over. He's there in the doorway — tall, smooth, dark. A living shadow in black T-shirt and black jeans. He must have come in so quietly. Padding like a cat.

He strolls down the steps towards me, half smiling.

"Just let yourself in, did you?"

I'm gabbling, sounding foolish. "Sorry, Luke. Yeah, I know. Sorry. The door was open and — um —"

"And you just walked in. Rude girl."

His eyes are cold. There's no smile on his face now, no welcome in his voice. He lifts his phone, thumbs some icon or other, and the door behind him slides smoothly shut.

"Technically, Taz," he says, "you're an intruder."

I'm backing against the desk, heart thumping. "Look, I know... I... I..."

"I don't like that," he says, still coldly. "You don't just come here when you like, I said. *You wait for an invitation.*"

He steps forward, closing the gap between us. His face is dark, eyes gleaming.

"So," he says, in a voice that makes me tremble with fear. "Now you've got to pay the price."

CHAPTER 6

MIND GAMES

"Luke, I'm sorry!"

I am almost screaming, backed up against the TV screens. They are uncomfortably warm. Their ghostly light plays over my face.

He comes right up close to me, and then his face suddenly breaks into a grin.

"Don't look so worried!" he says. "What did you think I was going to do?"

I glance away for a second, then try to look at him confidently. I'm still shaking. "I don't know," I admit.

"When I say pay the price," he says, "I just mean a sort of… entry fee. Close your eyes."

This really wasn't a good idea. I should have asked him first. I should have contacted him.

He kisses me before I have a chance to realise what's happening. He tastes hot and sweet.

Oh, blimey.

I open my eyes to see him smiling.

"See," he says, "that wasn't so bad as entry fees go."

OK… That was different. It wasn't *tender*, exactly, but he knew what he was doing.

"Yeah," I say, trying to sound casual, as if it means nothing, as if it has left me totally unaffected. "Thanks for that."

Look at the circles he moves in. He's *Eva Horton's* son, for goodness' sake. He could probably ask

her to put him in touch with,
I dunno, Chloe Moretz or Selena Gomez if
he wanted.

I admit I've been a bit slow with this kind
of thing. We're talking two kisses ever. Ryan
Barraclough (oh, God, why, *why?*) at Grace's
party in Year 10, when it was late and I didn't
really care. And Matt Delamere, who was a much
better option, after the Year 11 leavers' do. In the
upper science corridor, where nobody would be
watching. Shy boy. Almost too nice for me.

Oh, and Grace offered once, just in case, but I
let her down gently. Girls aren't for me, I know
that much.

Luke's not a git like Ryan Barraclough, or a shy,
cute boy like Matt Delamere. He's… well, he's
just Luke.

Dangerous, deep, mysterious Luke.

"Ever played I Spy?" he says. "When you were
a kid?"

"Course," I say. "On long boring car journeys."

He nods up at the screens. "Well, this… this is the fun version."

He backs away, beckoning. I follow him to the computer desk.

Have some self-respect, Tasmin, I say to myself. *You are not a dog. You don't do "heel"*. Halima and Grace would be looking disgustedly at me right now.

"How have you got all this?" I ask, with a mixture of fascination and disgust.

Luke presses his fingertips together, swivelling back and forth on his chair.

"I had three months alone here," he said, and looks up, smiling, spreading his hands. "And a lot of money, and I'm very clever. What can I say?"

I look at him in astonishment. "But people have bought these apartments. They… they really don't know?"

He laughs, mocking. "Oh, yes. Let me tell you about the people who bought them. Including," and here he points a finger at me, like he's aiming a gun, *"your mother."*

"Yes," I say guardedly. "My mother." I have to say it, even though it's not the first time I've had the thought. "Have you spied on *me*?"

He grins. "Relax. There aren't cameras in all the apartments. I didn't get round to yours."

I decide to believe him. For now.

"So," he goes on, "the kind of people who buy these apartments. They don't do all the legwork themselves, Taz. They don't look through property websites like normal people."

"They don't?" I suppose I have never really given this a lot of thought.

"No. They don't spend their weekends cooing over bathrooms and going, 'Ooh, isn't that one nice, Jeffrey?' and 'Ooh, yes, Demelza, that .

one's *charming*. What a *pleasing aspect* it has.' Those people who want to seem posher than they are. No, Taz, the people who bought these apartments *got people to do it for them.*"

"Right," I say, feeling stupid.

Of course they do.

Mum doesn't do her own shopping, washing, cleaning or accounts. It makes sense that she outsources a whole load of other stuff too.

"And there's guff in the contracts, sure," Luke carries on, "about security and safety and modern computer-controlled facilities. Oh, yeah. They love all that. They just don't understand it. They don't give a damn about what it means."

"Are people really that dim?" I ask with a grin.

"Mostly," says Luke. He has produced something out of thin air, like a magician. Another little shiny card like the one he gave me, only this one is red rather than black. "Know what this is?"

I shake my head.

"Again, something that's only possible with the tech. This is a master key. Gets into any apartment in the block."

Including ours, I think with a shiver, and try to let the thought pass.

"If the place had old-fashioned keys and bolts, it would be 20 times harder." Luke sniggers. "The more advanced the tech, the easier it is to screw it up. Now watch this."

Luke lunges at the keyboard, stabs at one of the keys.

All 320 screens suddenly make up one big one, a huge cinema-sized picture dominating the room. I gasp. It's showing a crisp, clear, hi-def image of one of the lifts.

"Look at all the *fun* we can have," says Luke softly.

And that's where it begins.

CHAPTER 7

BIG IRON

Two hours later.

"There!" I say.

Luke darts across the room, slams his hands down on the desk. "Oh, yes! We have lift-off!"

For two hours we've been waiting, bantering, drinking bottled water and Coke, watching the lift image. Two hours. Because this creepy, creaky apartment-block is half-empty at the moment, there hasn't been much sign of any action.

But now, two figures have entered the lift and pressed one of the buttons. A boy with red hair and glasses, and a tall long-haired, skinny woman in a shiny raincoat.

I suddenly realise.

"It's James!"

"Who?" Luke looks irritated that I have information which he doesn't.

"That boy who hangs around. And that must be his mum."

Luke glares at me. "Do you like him?"

I shrug. I barely know him. "I'm not sure," I reply. "Not really. Oh, I don't know."

Luke smiles. His hand hovers over the keyboard. Then it flickers over several keys and some digital readouts come up on the screen.

"They're in Lift 7," he says. "On the west side of the tower. Right…"

"What are you going to do?" I ask. I am curious, but also breathless with excitement. I am shaking. My mouth is dry.

It's like some deadly computer game where I'm waiting for him to make his next move. Only this is real. The place is real, the images are real, the people are real.

"Ever heard the expression, 'lights, camera, action'?" he says.

"Yeah."

"How about no lights?" Luke taps a key.

On the screen, I see the lights flicker and go off in the lift. And I go cold, remembering it happening to me.

James and his mum are looking at each other, worried. James has his phone out and is using the flashlight app.

"And now — no action!" says Luke with a grin. He taps another key.

The lift judders, and they stagger, open-mouthed.

I can't hear anything, but I can imagine the screeching of gears, the sound of tortured metal.

This is cruel. And I feel a thrill.

I hate myself. But I am enjoying this.

"So," Luke says, taking a thoughtful sip of water. "How long shall we leave them there?"

Five minutes pass.

***

I can see James's mum pressing the alarm button, talking into the grille. I'm actually impressed by how calm she is being.

"Will that do anything?" I ask Luke, nodding at what the woman is doing.

"Not now, it won't. I've deactivated the channel between Lift 7 and the callout service."

"Callout service? What, so there's no maintenance team in the tower?"

Luke grins. "Don't be daft. The contract's owned by a company based three miles away. It would take them half an hour to get an engineer here in London traffic, even if James's mummy could be heard." He chuckles. "Amazing what fun you can have with the right knowledge."

I fold my arms and scowl. I'm starting to feel bad. James isn't horrible, he's just a bit weird. "All right, stop it now. Give them the lights back, at least."

"What a kind little thing you are," says Luke. "When we rule the world together, you'll be wanting to spare all my enemies."

"Seriously. Luke. Come on." A thought occurs to me. "How are you doing all this, anyway?"

"The place is run by a clunky old mainframe computer. 'State of the art', they call it. 'Bit of a state', I call it. Seriously, I've never met a big iron that couldn't be hacked."

"Big iron?" I repeat, confused.

"Sorry. It's what the geeks call a massive computer. And this one? The security's so 1990s it may as well be using Windows NT."

"They told my mum security was *impregnable*," I argue. I remember the word. Reminded me of *pregnant*. Security so good it was better than the Pill. That's what I took from that.

"Yeah, and they said the *Titanic* was unsinkable."

"Are you doing it all off there?" I nod at his sleek black laptop, trying not to sound too impressed.

"To get whatever you want in life, you need at least one of three weapons. More money than your enemies, better tech than them, or better brains. That'll get you pretty much anything you want in life." Luke gives me a dazzling grin. "Me? I've got all three."

I look up at the screen. James is going stir-crazy now, pacing up and down, thumping the walls. His mum's trying to calm him down. She's gesturing at the phone on the wall. Probably saying she can't get a connection. (To the maintenance team three miles away, who'd take half an hour to get here.) James is waving his phone and pointing at it. Clever boy. But no — he's shaking his head, putting his hand to his forehead. Either he can't get a signal, or the battery's gone, or something else has happened.

"Luke, come on. This is cruel."

He laughs. "Say please."

"*Please*, Luke! It's not nice."

I hate myself for playing along, for *obeying* him like that. But I'd have hated myself even more if I'd allowed his little game to continue, even for another minute.

"Oh, all right," he says grumpily, and taps a key.

On the big screen, the lift lights up. It begins moving again, and James and his mum exchange relieved looks. A few seconds later, the doors open and they get out at their floor.

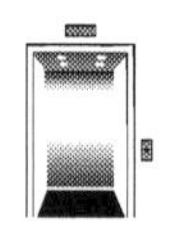

CHAPTER 8

TRICK OR TREAT

"Are you all right, darling?" my mother asks, checking her hair and earrings in the mirror.

I look up from my phone, smiling. "Why wouldn't I be?"

"You seem more cheerful," she says, hoisting her bag on to her shoulder. "Right. I'm off. Look after yourself. Lots of food in the fridge."

She blows me a kiss, and with a swirl of blue hair and a cloud of Chanel, she is out of the door. Off to catch a taxi to the airport. She's going to Paris for a week's conference, she says, on 'Beauty Blogging and Fashion in the New Media'.

Only I have looked this conference up online, and I know it only lasts three days. So, for the rest of the week, my mum is going to be doing other stuff in Paris.

She can stay for two weeks as far as I'm concerned.

I think she's got a bloke in Paris. She never mentions it, but I've picked up on the signs. Sneaky texts, new French clothes, expensive presents being delivered. I'm not stupid.

***

It's been a few days since Luke and I played our trick on James and his mum in the lift. And we've done more since then.

I've seen James skulking around, looking at me in that sneaky way. He's tried to watch me as I do my sketching — even tried to take photos of me.

I needed fresh air then, so I went outside. But of course, there's nothing much happening outside to speak of. Just a lot of scrubby wasteland, a hot smell of petrol and tarmac, and a loud dual carriageway beyond.

I could see the Olympic Park buildings shimmering in the heat — with nothing like the same aura of glamour they had back in 2012.

It was so depressing I had to go back in. The sweet cool air of Avalon Tower seemed almost a relief.

***

I go to the lift at the instructed time. A text beeps in on my phone and I look at it:

Darling. Everything wonderful here. Hope all is well.

I snort, and consider replying with something sarcastic. I don't, though. All right, my mum's annoying, but I don't want to spoil her time with Pierre or Jean-Jacques or whatever his name is. Mum deserves it at her age.

I hear a sound behind me and I whirl around. A figure hiding behind one of the pot-plants.

I sigh, fold my arms. "I can see you, James. No need to hide."

He steps out. His freckled face looks harder, colder. Not quite as gormless.

"I'd be careful if I were you," he says. "Those things aren't as reliable as you might think."

My heart skips a beat. Does he know something? Suspect something?

"Oh, really?" I say airily. "I've never had any trouble."

"That's not what I've heard," says James, and leans against the wall with a sly grin.

The lift pings. The doors open. I hesitate.

"Well, off you go," James says. "Going to do more sketching?"

"Y — yeah," I say quickly, grateful that he's provided me with a lie. Sighing with relief, I step into the lift.

The doors begin to rumble shut and I give him a silly, cute wave. "Bye, James."

"You forgot your sketchbook," he says knowingly.

And the doors slide shut.

I curse quietly. "It's… it's still up there!" I call, but I've no idea if he will hear me. Or believe me.

I insert my black card. The lift begins the smooth climb to Floor 41.

***

Luke is sitting with his feet on the desk. He hears me come in, raises a hand in greeting.

The screen is big again, showing one single camera. A young woman is pacing up and down her living-room, looking agitated.

"Apartment 37," he says. "Our occupant here has had no water or electricity for five hours."

"I recognise her," I say, squinting at the screen.

"Yeah, she's a soap actress. Tasha Livingstone. From *Scotland Street*?"

"Oh, yes," I say, trying to sound knowledgeable, although I have never watched more than a few minutes of *Scotland Street*.

This is the kind of thing we've done for the past few days. Well, Luke has done it, and I've kind of gone along with it, I suppose. Pranks, tricks, things to annoy and irritate people who have no idea that they're being watched.

OK, so — the list of crimes:

Luke's got access to the database of every occupant. (I wonder if that's how he knew my name.) So we know exactly who we're playing tricks on. Everything about them.

He says he can't get into their online details — yet — but I wonder if it's only a matter of time.

We can get into their heads, though.

We've played with the lifts, lights, heating, water. Amazing how it can mess with people's heads when these things seem to go wrong for no reason.

On the second day — I don't know how he did this one — he filled Apartment 88, where a sour-faced businesswoman called Amanda lives, with balloons. Every inch of the place. Every room, right up to the doorway. I suppose it must have taken a stupidly expensive online order and a whole day's work. It was worth it to see her livid red face as she popped each one with her pen, growling and grunting. I watched with my arms draped around Luke, as we laughed together.

Harmless, right?

On the third day, we made the lights strobe in Apartment 113, causing a woman called Becky

McKee to drop an entire lasagne on her kitchen floor, narrowly missing her foot. Luke recorded the footage of the lasagne explosion and played it back in slow motion.

Yeah, harmless.

On the fourth day, Luke told me he'd been watching a businessman called Nicholas Watts, who lives on Floor 5. Watts is a dull sort of guy. Married to a quiet woman who seems to stay at home all day. He leaves early in the morning and comes home after seven every evening. They seem happy enough. Or at least they did, until Luke managed to get the footage of Nicholas Watts visiting his twenty-year-old mistress, the daughter of the family in Apartment 72. And Luke somehow hacked the TVs in their apartment — all seven of them — so that they showed Watts kissing the girl in the car park before she sped away in a gleaming red Porsche.

"He bought her that," Luke said softly. "Can you believe it? With the family money. Wifey had no idea."

That comment made me look at him closely, watching his face in shadow, seeing how hard and angry he looked.

I wondered, not for the first time, how Luke really felt about his mother's very public private life. Eva Horton's been through a lot of younger men, everyone knows that. Is *that* what this is all about? Luke's angry revenge on the world? It's hard to see him as a sort of moral force. Cheating is not very nice, sure, but I can't see Luke getting hot under the collar about it otherwise.

Harmless, yeah?

Maybe not so much anymore.

I'm worried now.

Worried about what he'll come up with next.

CHAPTER 9

CLOSED CIRCUIT

"Give her the water back, at least," I say, watching Tasha Livingstone pace up and down in the dim red emergency lighting. She is shouting into her phone. Looks as if she is swearing. A lot. She kicks a chair over.

Luke laughs. "No. This is too much fun."

I fold my arms. I want to challenge him. "Yeah, but it's all easy, isn't it?"

He turns slowly towards me, narrowing his eyes in the flickering light. He lowers his head, cheekbones sharp, dark hair falling over his eyes.

"What's that supposed to mean?"

"Well," I say, my voice level and confident. "You've not really tested yourself, have you? Or me. I mean, yeah, anyone can sit up here playing stupid tricks with a computer. Using a master key when you know people are out. What about doing something *dangerous*? Something that would really get you in trouble if you were caught?"

Luke raises his eyebrows. His smile doesn't slip. "What did you have in mind?" he asks.

So I tell him.

***

Over the next few days, items start to go missing from various apartments in Avalon Tower. Small things at first. Keys, ornaments, even kitchen items. Then bigger things — smartphones, laptops, tablets. And jewellery, including some of my mum's stuff from her mystery lover.

They always disappear when the owner is out. But there's never any sign of forced entry, or any other indication that anyone's been in the apartment. It's almost as if someone had access to the apartments, and some way of knowing when they would be empty.

***

I look at the plastic crates piled high with the stolen objects. There are three of them now.

It's late. I don't know how late. It's dark outside — I can see the city lights spread out beneath Luke's circular window.

"We're going to give all this back, right?" I say to him.

Luke leans on the desk and looks me up and down. "Supposing we don't?" he says. "Supposing this is just the start?"

"Yeah, but, come on, Luke. You don't need to nick stuff. You can just ask Mummy for a bit extra, can't you?"

He looks angry for a moment. "Don't always bring this back to my mother, Tasmin."

"Sorr-*eee*," I say sarcastically. "No, but, come on — really. I think we should stop. We've had our fun." I decide to say what else has been on my mind for a few days too. "And I think you should take the cameras out. One by one, when people aren't at home. It isn't really very fair to keep spying on them like this."

He stands up straight, very slowly and deliberately, and walks around me. I swallow hard, closing my eyes tightly.

He is right behind me, his breath in my ear. "Are you trying to tell me what to do, Taz? Don't tell me what to do."

"I just think —"

"Well, *don't!*" His voice is a whiplash, making me jump.

"Sorry," I say, and my voice comes out as a croak.

He pulls the chair out, gestures. "Sit down, Taz."

Trembling, I obey.

"Do you know, Taz," he says, "how easy it is to make people believe stuff they half want to believe anyway?"

He taps at the keyboard. The face of a young woman comes up. She is blonde and chubby with a sad expression. She looks as if she is wearing some kind of red uniform top, made out of polyester.

"I've no idea who that is," I say.

"I know," he says. "I'm about to tell you… Keeley Wragg. Works here as a cleaner. You won't see her. One of the invisible people. Been and gone by the time you surface from your pit."

I scowl and fold my arms. "Is there any point to this?"

Luke holds up a hand, smiles. "Patience," he says. "Now, the thing about the cleaners here is that they're on a contract. It comes with the maintenance fee all the residents pay. So they don't just do the public areas, they do all the apartments as well. Which means they have…" Luke waggles his red plastic card in my face, "a master key."

"Where are you going with this, Luke?" I'm really uneasy now.

"As of yesterday," Luke says, "Keeley Wragg has been suspended from her job. Know why?"

I shake my head dumbly. "She missed a bit?"

"Ha ha. But no. She was found by the supervisor with several items in her bag belonging to residents. Electronic goods and jewellery, mainly. Oh, now, of course, Miss Wragg protests her innocence, but…" Luke sighs, spreads his hands.

"When the evidence is there..."

I gawp at him in horror. "A plant?"

"Oh, such dramatic language. But yes, if you like. A *plant*." He taps the master key-card. "Amazing what you can do with one of these," he says, slipping it into his pocket.

"But that's not fair! That woman's going to lose her job because of your little games!"

Luke grins smugly. "I know." He lifts his eyebrows, spreads his arms out as if to embrace the entire tower-block. "I'm only just beginning to realise the extent of my power."

You know what? He actually says it like he believes it.

And now, I feel really sick. The whole place seems to tilt as I stand up, and my legs feel wobbly. But anger gives me strength.

"You're not God," I snap at him. "You're not some, some… devious mega-villain holed up in your HQ, battling arch-enemies. God, I thought you were cool, but… no. You're a saddo, Luke. Playing around with people's lives because you think you're better than them."

"Oh, names, names! You really hurt me, Taz."

I don't let myself be put off. "You're like one of those loser dudes who spend all their time in Mum and Dad's basement, looking at creepy websites and playing *GTA* and *Call of Duty* non-stop." I turn and start to walk for the door. "We need to come clean. Tell the police it was all a game. They'll understand if we own up."

His *Star Trek* door to the outside world slides shut before I have time to get up the steps.

My heart is pounding, my throat dry. I turn and look at him. He's standing there with his phone. He shrugs, smiles.

"Sorry," he says. "I kind of knew you were going to do that."

I rummage for my phone, pull it out. For some reason, although I know it's fully charged, the screen is blank and it won't work.

I put it back in my pocket, advance on Luke with what I hope is a cold, hard expression.

"Be very careful, Taz."

"Or *what*?" I snap.

I regret that the minute I've said it.

The photo of the cleaner disappears. For a second the screen is totally blank, and then something appears. Not a photo. Letters and numbers, white on a black background. At first, I don't realise what I am looking at.

And then I do.

My mother's name, and the name of her company. And underneath, scrolling white numbers with dates. Money in and out.

The actual numbers mean nothing to me. What's 'a lot of money'? I really don't know. If I put a figure on it, I'd just sound stupid. But… it looks like there's a lot going on there. Money going in and out. A column on the right getting bigger and bigger.

"Your mum's profit and loss accounts," says Luke casually. "It took a while, but… I got there in the end. My, my, isn't she doing well? In fact — let's take a look, shall we?"

"Don't do this."

He ignores me. A six-figure sum in euros appears on the screen, bold and huge, taking up almost the whole space.

It's so big. The numbers and the money. It just looks ridiculous.

"Your mother's personal net wealth," says Luke, "as declared to her accountants at the end of the last tax year. Not bad. Not bad at all. That'll buy a lot of trips to Paris, Taz. Nice clothes and food and trinkets and holidays. Oh, and a *very* posh school for you for the next two years. And university fees? No problem."

"Luke —"

"But what if I were to do *this*?" he says — and with a click, the six-figure sum starts counting down.

One euro less each second.

Like a massive countdown.

Money disappearing from my mum's bank account.

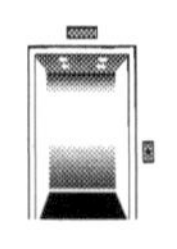

CHAPTER 10

FINAL TEST

"What are you doing? How are you doing this?"

He can't really have access to Mum's bank. He *can't.* It must be some horrible trick. Something he's doing with the computer.

But then, he hacked a mainframe. A 'big iron'. He controls the cameras, lifts, lights and water.

He just might be able to do this.

This could just be real.

"I can't keep you here, obviously," says Luke with a wry grin. He taps his phone and the door slides open. Beyond, the black doors to the lobby click open too. "But if you run — the euros go down."

The numbers on the screen keep counting down.

"Now, I'm not taking this for myself," says Luke. "Perish the thought. I don't need money. But the Peckham Cat Protection League are going to *love* this generous donation from Bel Jessop."

I look from Luke, to the screen, to the door and back to Luke again. My throat is dry. I feel dizzy.

I suddenly have the germ of an idea.

"All right, Luke," I say, slipping closer to him, holding eye contact. "Very good. Very powerful. I'm impressed."

He seems surprised. "You are?"

"Yeah." I grin, and giggle. "OK… Maybe I was wrong. I do want excitement in my life."

And as I speak, my hand steals to his back pocket, caresses, slips out again.

I chance it. I pull away.

"What are you doing?" he snarls.

I give him a cute little wave, running for the open door with the master key in my hand.

***

In the lift, the doors slide shut. The lift begins to drop.

I hold my breath, but it's already too late. His voice comes out of the speaker.

"I really wouldn't do anything stupid, Taz. Come back and we'll talk about this together."

"No way! I can't believe I trusted you! Liked you!"

The lift judders. The digital display of the floor numbers flickers between 30 and 29. The lights flash on and off.

I press myself against the wall. I've been here before. I'm not going to let myself be scared by this.

"I know your tricks now!" I shout up at where I guess the camera might be. "They don't frighten me anymore!"

For a second, the lift is plunged into darkness, and then it creaks to a complete halt.

I listen. Over the thudding of my heart I can hear the creak of straining cables, the clunking of gears echoing up and down the shaft.

I'm between Floors 30 and 29. That's a hell of a long way down.

I don't know how long I am there in the darkness, suspended, the lift not moving but creaking alarmingly.

But then, the lights flicker back on, and the lift starts to move again. Very, very slowly descending to Floor 20.

The doors judder open and, gulping the air in relief, I rush across the hall to our door. I shove my key-card in the slot.

For a second I think it's not working, but that's just me being impatient. The door slides open.

"Mum?" I call hopefully, just in case she is home early. But no — our apartment is quiet and empty, just as I left it.

My phone's still dead. I grab the landline and wonder, for a second, who to call. Mum? The police?

As I am standing there wondering, the lights flicker in our apartment.

I drop the phone.

And I hear his voice. It comes out of the TV.

"You know I'm just teasing you, Taz. I can stop you at any time."

The lights go off. Seconds later the reddish-orange emergency back-up lighting kicks in, and I breathe a sigh of relief.

"Pretty-boy thinks he's got it all sussed," says a different voice from right behind me.

I gasp and turn around.

***

A figure emerges from our kitchen. I can't see who it is at first, until he steps out of the shadows. Then I sigh with relief.

"James. What the hell are you doing in here?"

"Waiting for you," he says.

I back away into the wall. "How did you get in?"

I realise he's holding a laptop. He points to it. "Pretty-boy upstairs isn't the only one with tech skills."

He sets the computer on our kitchen worktop and starts typing frantically, the soft lights reflecting in his glasses. Curious, I come round to see what he's doing. I can't make sense of it, though. Just a lot of numbers and symbols.

Oh, yeah, coding. Something I never did at school.

"You see," he says, "Luke thinks he's the only one who can hack systems. That's where he's wrong."

The red lights buzz and flicker for a second.

"You?" I say. "You mean…"

"I did say I was getting a place at college sponsored by LumiTech, right? You sounded like you knew what I meant. But you didn't seem that impressed. So I didn't push it."

The conversation comes back to me, now. Guiltily, I realise that I wasn't all that interested in hearing anything James had to say at the time.

"So LumiTech is…"

"Specialist training for IT experts," he says. "Mr Cheekbones might fancy himself as a bit of a star in that department. But believe me, he's just an amateur."

"James," I say in awe, "are you telling me you *know* all about Luke?"

James gives me a little pitying, sideways look. He continues tapping furiously on the keyboard.

"But… in the lift… You looked freaked out! You're saying you knew what was happening all along?"

"Had to let him think he was winning," says James, with a cheeky grin. "My poor mum."

I don't feel quite so bad now for letting Luke trap them in the lift all that time. Well, I feel bad for James's mum, perhaps, but not for him.

Everything's happened so quickly. I can barely take it in.

"Look, James," I say awkwardly, "I may have been a bit… off with you."

He waves a hand. "People always are. I don't always pick up on social cues. Don't worry about it."

"Right." I have to ask the obvious question. "What are you doing there?"

"Trying to get into Mr Alpha Male's system," he says. "And…" He steps back from the laptop and gives himself a little clap of triumph. "Succeeding."

"Is he really draining my mum's bank account?" I ask.

James pulls a sorry-looking face. "Could be. But… probably not, I'd say. It's a very easy thing to mimic. Especially if you don't know how much is actually in there to begin with."

I feel myself blush. I realise I actually have no idea.

"He's not the only one who can hack into cameras, either. You see, he might have thought he'd deleted all the recording of you and him sneaking into various apartments. But actually, it's really hard to *destroy* data. It just goes somewhere else."

My eyes open wide. "You mean…?"

James nods. "All safely stored away. I emailed the videos as a zip-file to the police about an hour ago. Got a response too. It seems they're *very* interested in anything to do with Avalon Tower."

James presses a key with a final flourish.

"There you go. That should give him something to think about."

I almost forgot.

I remember that moment I said goodbye to Luke. In the rush of escape, I had forgotten. I reach into my pocket and pull out his red master key. It gleams softly in the dim light.

He nods, impressed. "That should clinch it."

And then I hear a *clunk* — unmistakably the sound of the apartment door locking itself. Then, the windows all start to darken on their own, tinting to brown and then black, until they are totally dark and we can't see a thing out of them.

"I know what you're doing," says Luke's voice from the TV speaker. *"I know what you're doing and I can stop you."*

I look at James in alarm.

"I'm working on it," he says. "I'm locked out of the system."

A click and a clunk comes from the ceiling. And then I feel drips of water. I look up in alarm.

"Sprinklers!" says James.

We run for cover under the kitchen worktop as the cold water from the sprinklers hammers down. A second later, the howl of the fire-alarm fills the air.

I think I can smell smoke.

We just have to hope now. Hope that James has done enough. Even though it's going to get me into trouble too, I don't care anymore.

The emergency red lighting dims once. It flickers, flares and then goes out completely, plunging the apartment into darkness.

In the distance, I hear the sound of police sirens.

ABOUT THE AUTHOR

Daniel Blythe is the author of 20 books, including several of the *Doctor Who* novels, as well as *Shadow Runners* and *Emerald Greene and the Witch Stones*. He is originally from Maidstone, but now lives with his wife and teenage children in Yorkshire. He has been published in 12 countries including the USA, Germany and Brazil, and he has led writing days and workshops in over 400 schools.